Ten Gold Medals
Glory or Freedom

By Isaac Dostis

An Adventure Based on a True Story of Escape From Greece During WWII

Edited by Marcia Haddad Ikonomopoulos

Published for
The Association of Friends of Greek Jewry
by Bloch Publishing Co.

Published for The Association of Friends of Greek Jewry
By Bloch Publishing

ISBN 0-8197-0770-8 HC

Graphic Design by Amy R. Feigenbaum

Cover by Padraic Fitzgerald

Printed in the United States of America

Dedicated to ISAAC COHEN
An exceptional athlete
An exceptional uncle
A great human being

ACKNOWLEDGEMENTS

There are many people who have made this book possible. If it weren't for the sharing of my Aunt Dora and Uncle Isaac's story of rescue, much of what is in this book would have remained untold.

It takes a lot more than just knowing the story to make a book happen. Act 1 Presentations is a company that works with moral courage and each member, Diana Sunrise, Jane Ryan, David Graber and Sheldon Greenspan, all believe and support this undertaking.

I want to thank others who believe in this endeavor – Marc Fox, Karen Cressman, Noreen Munnelly, Connie Johnson, Nancy Musick, Christine Wang, Paul Dames, Bonnie Haberman, R. Blaustein, Roselle Kalosieh, Irma Jenne, Joan and Ron Porath, Mary Scripture, Julia Dunn, Owen Cowitt, Sol Rubin, Mary Mosquera, Bob Tavaska, Sandra Barty, Cece Dorough, Ann Goldstein, Lexie Demirali, Jerry and Judy Cotton, Bill and Mary Cressman, Kathy Speck, John and Deborah Conow, Candice Azzara, Gordon and Doris Firestein, Max and June Kerman, Bunny Barnes, Martin Contzius, Rev. Nancy Forsberg, Clark and Mary Creech, Ari Connerty-Singer and his parents, Mary and Frank, Charles and Mary Kayhart, Bonnie Dougherty, the folks at Notre Dame of Mt. Carmel Church, Linda Schmider, The Center for Holocaust Studies in Lincroft, NJ, Eileen and Joe Caccavale, Jean Zipser, Bernadette Johnson, Phyllis Schleifer, Jeff and Nicole Hopkins, Sy Rotter, Richard and Bunny

Goldstein, Ike and Ruth Chicurel, Jerry and Ruth Maletsky, Hilary Talis, B. Nice! Productions, and Ray and Coleen Bock.

I am grateful to my friend, Fred Storfer, who has come to my aid, oh, so many times.

I also want to thank Padraic Fitzgerald for drawing some of the illustrations with a grant from the Arts Council of the Morris Area in New Jersey.

This project could not have happened without the help and support of Marcia Haddad Ikonomopoulos, the President of The Association of Friends of Greek Jewry, who is more than just an editor, but a friend and associate who shares my belief in making the Holocaust in Greece more visible.

A special thanks to David Groenlund who came to our apartment every morning and with tears in his eyes listened to the story of Laíki and the medals unfold.

Last, but certainly not least in any way, I want to thank my wife, Diana, who has traveled this path with me for so many loving years. She helps and expands my vision in so many different ways.

Isaac Dostis

ADDITIONAL ACKNOWLEDGEMENTS

In a venture of this kind there are always special people, who because of their financial, emotional or spiritual support, enable the project to take root and to blossom.

The Association of Friends of Greek Jewry would like to acknowledge and thank our loyal supporters who aided in the publication of *Ten Gold Medals: Glory or Freedom:* Katherine & Maurice Askinazi, Regina Battino, Steven Battino, Isaac & Joyce Ben-Ezra, Mary & Stan Calof, Lena Casuto, Gabriel Cohen, Isaac Cohen, Harvey Colchamiro, Jesse Colchamiro, Leonard Colchamiro, Joshua Dostis, Robert Dostis, Rita Elias, Elias M. Eliasof, Jeanne Eliasoff, Sandra Fox, Hy & Lil Genee, Barbara Gharemani, Corinna Gittleman, Dr. Simon & Perla Halegoua, Denise & Irwin Hametz, Mark Hametz, Lou Harris, Dr. & Mrs. Sol Hasson, Joseph Josephs, Vivian Kominos & Elliot Smith, Lois Ledner, Stella Levi, Bernard Levy, David Levy, Jeanette Levy, Mat Levy, Louis Menashe, Philip & Barbara Moss, Annette & Irving Myones in memory of Henry Miles, Samuel Nahoum, Belle Negrin Davis, David A. Negrin, David S. Negrin, David Negrin, Shirlee Paganetti, Jerry Pardo, Michael Pessah, Gladys Russo, Eli Samuels, Cantor Rita Shore, Mel & Annette Skriloff, Dorothy & Ruben Stein, Randi & Gerry Vagelatos, Samuel Vitoulis, David R. Yohanna, & Renee Yomtov Rosenthal.

In addition, I wish to personally thank Ronnie Dellen, Renee Yomtov Rosenthal and Corrina Gittleman for their invaluable editorial help, and Nikos Stavroulakis for his historical insights.

A special thanks to Amy Feigenbaum whose patience knows no bounds and whose talent is only surpassed by her generosity of spirit.

Finally, our eternal gratitude to Charles Bloch, a man of integrity for whom the success of a publication encompasses more than just financial profits.

Marcia Haddad Ikonomopoulos

EDITOR'S INTRODUCTION

From 1939 to 1945, as the horrors of the Holocaust spread across Europe, there would be millions of innocent victims. Of the eleven million who lost their lives, victims of the Nazis, six million were Jews. Of those six million, 67,000 were Greek Jews. While the story of the Holocaust has been told many times since, the world is still trying to come to terms with the unexplainable horrors, and many still do not know of the losses in Greece.

In 1940, when the Italian and German armies invaded Greece, there were close to 78,000 Jews living on Greek soil. The Jews, some of whom dated their presence in Greece back to the time of Alexander the Great, lived throughout the country, in cities, villages and on many of the islands. They played an active role in the economy and were considered full citizens of Greece ever since it became a modern country in the 19th century.

Sixty years after the crimes of the Holocaust, we all realize that there is still much to learn. For this reason, here in the United States, and in countries throughout Europe, the Holocaust is taught in schools. It is hoped that the lessons learned from the Holocaust will prevent another 'holocaust', whether it be one based on religion, race or ethnic differences.

It is with these two goals in mind, teaching the Holocaust as a means of teaching tolerance and educating the world on the 'Greek' Holocaust, that we have published *Ten Gold*

Medals: Glory or Freedom. It is our hope that it will be read by children throughout the world and that a generation will grow up knowing of our losses.

Isaac Dostis, an actor, filmmaker and educator, has dedicated his life to teaching tolerance and telling the story of the Greek Holocaust. His own family, Greek-speaking Jews who lived in small cities like Ioánnina, Arta, Préveza and Pátras in Greece, suffered tremendous losses. There were also those among them, like the Cohen family in *Ten Gold Medals: Glory or Freedom,* who owe their lives to courageous Greek Christians who risked their own lives to save them. *Ten Gold Medals: Glory or Freedom* tells both sides of the story, the suffering and sacrifices, and the triumphs of survival, in a way that can be appreciated and understood by children.

Marcia Haddad Ikonomopoulos
Editor

THE WAR COMES HOME

The rumble of the tanks scared Laíki* as he was playing in Athens outside the house. Since the war began, Laíki's family, the Cohens, had been living in Athens, using false names to hide their true identity. Laíki ran to his mother as fast as his eight-year-old legs would take him.

"Mama, Mama, they are here! They are here!" he shouted as he pointed out the window. Dora stopped her cooking, and with dishrag in hand, ran to her excited son and grabbed him by the mouth to quiet him. "Never say that again. We are one of them. We are one of them now! No one must know that we are Jews."

She could see the pain and fear in the little boy's eyes. When she let go of his mouth, he was bleeding. She didn't realize how she had hurt him. She had only been trying to protect

*Laíki: pronounced "<u>Lie</u>-key"

him. She wiped the blood quickly and bent down to hug him. Never would she hurt him again. Never.

Little Laíki with the big eyes was learning his lessons.

But to whom did these tanks belong? Who were the people Laíki's Mom was talking about when she said, "We are one of them now?"

It was 1943 and all of Europe was in the middle of a war. It was an ugly war and many people would die. A madman named Adolph Hitler wanted to rule the world and wanted only those who were like him to live in that world. He hated Jews and other people who were different from him. The people who joined him were called Nazis, the German initials of the Nationalist Socialist Party in Germany.

From 1939 to 1945 over eleven million people would be killed. Among them would be six million Jews who would die for no reason other than that they practiced a different religion. After it was all over, people would call this the Holocaust.

Jews lived in many different countries in Europe and Greece was one of them. Many people know that Jews from Russia, Poland and Germany were killed, but not many people know that there was a Holocaust in Greece where Laíki and his family lived.

The Nazis stormed through the countries of Europe quickly overtaking many democracies. They came to Greece in 1941.

Laíki and his family were Jews. To Hitler and the Nazis, Jews were different. The Cohen family would have to hide. They could not let anyone know that they were Jewish. To do so would be very dangerous.

The Rumble of the Tanks

Athens Synagogue on Melidoni Street where the round ups took place

Laíki left his mother's arms and ran into the bedroom. The small house where they were living belonged to a baker and his wife, Yiánni and Maria Panayotarákos, friends of the family who lived in the larger house in front.

Laíki fell onto the bed that he shared with his little sister, Zoítsa* and searched for his father's gold medals. Isaac Cohen, Laíki's father, had won the medals while competing in athletics in Greece.

He found all ten of them where he had left them, under his mattress in an old colorful bag. As he took them out, he could smell the fresh bread being baked across the yard. He looked out the window. He saw the baker, an older man with glasses, kneading some more dough. The baker looked up. Laíki's big eyes were all the baker saw.

Knowing what Laíki and his family were in need of, the baker motioned with a smile "not yet" and put up two fingers. The little boy knew what that meant. "Two hours is a long time to wait," Laíki thought disappointedly. He had to content himself with the shiny gold medals. His stomach would have to wait.

When the Nazis conquered Greece, Jews in Athens were told to come to their synagogues where they worshipped, and register their names and addresses. The Nazis wanted to know where all the Jews were living. Laíki's father, Isaac Cohen, refused to register his family.

Instead, he went into hiding and, with the help of the baker, proceeded to get false papers for the family. During the war, there was a shortage of food. The only way to get food for your

**Zoítsa: pronounced "Zo-eet-sa"*

family, if you lived in the city, was to get food stamps. Each family was allowed only a certain number of stamps. But you could not get stamps unless you had an identification card with your name and your picture on it. If you were Jewish, this could be very dangerous. Many Jews in Greece were able to get false cards with Christian names. The Chief of Police in Athens, Ángelos Evert, and the Archbishop of Greece, Damaskenós, helped them.

Laíki's real name was Bezalél. The Greek version of this Jewish name was Vassilákis. The family shortened it to Laíki. His sister's name, Joya became Zoítsa. His Mom retained her own first name, Dora, and his father Isaac Cohen became Yiórgo Hellás*.."

**Yiórgo Hellás: pronounced "Your-go Ell-ahs"*

The Baker and his wife with the Cohen Family

HELLAS

Nazi flag flies over Athens

Yiórgo Hellás was a joke that only Greeks would understand. It translates as "George, of Greece," but since George was King of Greece at the time, the joke really meant "George, The King."

Laíki's father, Isaac, was a tall, lean man. He had won ten gold medals in competitions in Greece. He was proud of his medals and so was Laíki.

Laíki carefully took the shiny coins out of the bag. His father told him that if Laíki wanted to keep them, he would have to take care of them — polish them and keep them safe, away from Zoítsa, his three-year-old sister.

Some of the medals still had the blue and white ribbons attached (blue and white are the colors of Greece's flag) and each had a man in the position of what the event was.

Laíki counted them as he had done so many times before. "Let's see. There are three for javelin," and he put them on one side of the bed. "There are three for running. Papa is very fast," he thought.

The other four were for broad jump, hurdles and discus. One had a chip in it and some were missing the ribbon holder, but other than that, all were bright and shiny, and all had the name of the country — Hellas [which means Greece] — on them. Making sure Zoítsa wasn't around, Laíki found a clean rag and started polishing. He felt happy again.

The people of Athens, the capital of Greece, felt very bad when the Nazis took over the city and installed their flag on the Acropolis in place of the Greek flag. The Acropolis was very important to Greeks. It was here, on top of one of the highest hills in Greece, that Ancient Greeks had built their temples to their gods. It was here, at the foot of the Acropolis, that democracy was born.

Laíki could see the new flag from his window. Instead of the familiar blue and white colors, it was now black and red.

And the language he heard from the soldiers with the guns and the tanks was German, not the national language—Greek.

Laíki's mother and father kept drilling him and Zoítsa about their names, their constantly changing address, their father's name, mother's name....

Laíki's world was being turned upside-down and he didn't understand all of it. He knew he didn't like it.

THE FIRST GOLD MEDAL

Late one Sunday afternoon, as Laíki was sitting in his room, he overheard voices at the front door. "Dora, don't worry," the neighbor said, "we won't say anything about your being Jewish."

"Thank you, Diamónda*, thank you," he heard his mother say sweetly. But as soon as Dora closed the door, she rushed into the bedroom with Zoítsa.

"Come on. Come on! We need to get dressed. We're leaving!" Dora yelled in a hushed voice, as she dragged the little girl into the room.

Laíki jumped up. "What happened?"

"What happened? What happened? Ask your sister." Dora quickly took some clothes out of a pile for the children to wear.

Laíki pointed to his sister. "Is she making us move again?"

He fell on his bed covering his almost crying eyes. He felt for the medals to make sure they were there under the mattress.

** Diamónda: pronounced "Dee-ah-mon-da"*

"Come on, come on, we must get ready to leave. Zoítsa come, put some clothes on top of the ones you have on."

Zoítsa was also on the verge of tears. Laíki turned on his bed. "What did she do?" he pleaded.

"Do you want to tell him, little girl?" Zoítsa was frozen. "She went to church with Diamónda's family which was fine, but when they all made the sign of the cross, they wondered why your sister didn't do it also." Dora looked at Zoítsa directly. "And what did you say when they asked you to make the sign? Tell your brother."

Zoítsa mumbled, "I said I couldn't because I was...Jewish." The tears finally came for the three-year-old.

"So," continued Dora, "We need to leave. We can't trust that Diamónda's children won't say anything."

When Isaac came home from trying to make money to feed the family, all three were ready to leave. Under the cover of darkness and wrapped with double and triple sets of clothing, they left for another safe house.

Before leaving, Isaac left one of his medals on the baker's windowsill, to say thank you. Laíki made sure the other nine medals were safe in the innermost portion of his clothing.

THE SECOND GOLD MEDAL

Walking the streets of Athens, in the cold winter weather, Laíki could see all the starving Greeks near Omónia Square and Sýntagma Square, two main squares in Athens. Jews needed to be careful. Everyone was suffering. If you turned a Jew in to the Germans, you could get sugar, coffee, and bread.

From a piece of paper the baker had given Isaac many weeks before, the family found someone willing to take them in for awhile. The only problem was that this safe house was run by the Greek Resistance Movement and had a short wave radio. The Greek Resistance Movement was trying to free Greece from the Germans. The short wave radio connected the Resistance Movement, patriots of Greece who were fighting the enemy, with each other, but its presence in the house could make it dangerous for the Cohen family.

"Come in, come in," Maria urged the weary family. "There is a room down in the basement near the radio transmitter. We'll have something to eat in a little while."

The Cohen family climbed down the ladder to the dark basement where a husky man with a mustache was hunched over the radio. Laíki could hear the crackling of the machine as they went about finding a mattress, a chair, a table. The man motioned the family to be quiet and stay as far away from him as possible.

That night, after dinner, the Cohens settled onto their mattress with the Greek partisan [Resistance Fighter] nearby. Laíki found a small bookcase where they all put their clothing and valuables. He put the colorful bag there too, behind everyone's few belongings.

Laíki was the first to open his eyes in the morning. Outside he saw snow! His eyes opened even wider. He only remembered snow once before in his life. But he felt safe with his family and the medals nearby.

He looked over at the radio. The man had fallen asleep, as well, and the radio was quiet. All of a sudden, noises started coming out of the transmitter. The man jumped in his seat and twisted some dials as he put his headset on.

Almost immediately, he dropped everything and ran to the ladder, climbed and lifted the door. "Maria," he shouted, "Maria! The German tanks are in the neighborhood. They are searching for the radio signal." Laíki's mouth was as wide open as his eyes.

"Shut the radio and hide it in the wall," Maria said urgently, "and get those Jews out of here! Quickly, quickly!"

The commotion woke Isaac and Dora up. They started gathering everything. "No, no," the man commanded as he came back down the ladder. "Leave everything. They will kill us all if they find you here. A radio is bad enough but Jews...."

Isaac took Zoítsa and climbed up the ladder. Laíki was pushed by his mother to follow. "But Mama...." "No buts. Hurry! Hurry!" Dora managed to get him up the ladder overcoming his protests.

Maria was already at the door, waiting. "It's snowing and cold but this is the only way," she said to Isaac quickly. "Here is a blanket. Go to the plateía* [square] and stay there for a while. When you see this front window open a bit, you'll know it is safe to come back," she instructed him.

Isaac wrapped the children up and the four walked the few blocks to the plateía, passing the search party, and sat on the cold grass. They had brought no food, no money and worst of all, Laíki worried about the medals he had left in the house.

The snow was letting up but their bellies were empty and their hearts were full of fear.

The morning passed slowly. The snow stopped but the wind continued as the four members of the Cohen family sat in the plateía. Soon the children started to complain about being hungry. Laíki heard his mother's stomach growl as he lay in her lap, huddled with Zoítsa against the cold.

Isaac went over to the house a few times but each time the window was shut. Finally, after a few hours he came up with a solution. He would go and knock on the door claiming he was looking for someone. If the Germans were there, he would apologize and say it must be the wrong house.

He left his family once again and quickly came to the house. He listened for any sounds. There weren't any. He looked at the window. Still closed. He took a deep breath and knocked.

**plateía: pronounced "plat-ee-a"*

Maria opened the door. "Where have you been?" she gasped. "We've been waiting for you to return." She pulled him into the hallway and closed the door.

After Isaac protested, Maria realized her mistake. With all the commotion, she had forgotten to open the window.

"But I have a surprise for you," she said, urging Isaac into the kitchen. There was another man sitting at the table. As he rose and turned, Isaac knew him immediately. They embraced with tears and with the usual Greek greeting — kisses on both cheeks.

"Kostas, my friend, my brother," murmured Isaac while in the embrace.

Kostas and Isaac were life-long friends having gone to school together in Préveza*, a small town on the western coast of Greece. They were on the same soccer team and they lived only two blocks away from each other. Their families were friends and shared holy days together—both Christian and Jewish.

When the war began, they lost touch with each other in Athens, as Kostas became a doctor and Isaac sold dry goods, mostly fabrics. Now, they were together again in one room.

"How did you find me?" asked Isaac, disbelieving that his friend of so many years was near him.

"Through the radio transmitter. We keep tabs on different safe houses. And when Maria described you and Dora and the children and the medals Laíki was showing off, I thought it might be you."

** Préveza: pronounced: "Preh-ve-za"*

Kostas Nikoláou

Isaac laughed and hugged his friend once more. “But, my friend, Maria tells me there is trouble,” continued Kostas.

“Yes,” Maria interrupted, “you must leave immediately. They say the Nazis will be back. They haven’t found our radio signal yet, but if they find you here as well....”

“I know,” Isaac said, completing the sentence, “finding a radio will get you to prison, finding a Jew will get you killed.”

“So,” continued Kostas, “go get the family. We’ll gather your belongings and take you to another house in Petroúpoli [a district in northern Athens away from the city center]. There I’m sure it will be safer.”

When the family was reunited in the house, Isaac left one of the medals for Maria as a remembrance. “That’s the least I can do,” he thought to himself.

THE THIRD GOLD MEDAL

The house in Petroúpoli was owned by Caliópe*, an old woman who had lost her husband in the war. She helped many Jews who passed through her house to safety.

Caliópe had an extra room. She was told to say that Isaac was a nephew from the war-torn areas of Greece. It certainly seemed much safer. With false papers, the family was able to walk the streets with less fear.

One day, a beggar came to the door and Isaac answered it. "Please, can you give me a few drachmas [the money of Greece] so I can buy some bread?", the man pleaded. "I haven't eaten for...." He stopped in the middle of his sentence.

"I know you!" he accused. "You are a Jew! You come from Préveza where I come from. You're a Jewish athlete. Give me money or I'll turn you into the police," he demanded.

** Caliópe: pronounced "Cal-ee-oh-peh"*

Laíki heard the commotion from the family's room and wondered how his father would handle it.

"Alright," Isaac said as easily as he could, "here is some money but promise me you won't come back."

"No, no," promised the beggar as he walked over to another house to beg again.

Laíki ran to his father. "Papa, what are you going to do?" Laíki asked worriedly as Isaac closed the door and leaned heavily against it. "I don't know, Pashá [an affectionate term meaning "prince"]. Let's hope this is the end of it. But promise not to tell your mother when she comes home with Zoítsa." Laíki nodded in agreement.

But in a few days, the beggar returned, now with a stubble of a beard. "Give me some money, Mr. Athlete Jew." Isaac knew that everyone in Greece was suffering and so he gave the beggar more drachmas with the promise that he wouldn't return.

"Papa, he's going to come again and again. We're going to have to move again," Laíki whined when they were alone.

"Shhh, my son, I have a plan, but I will need one of the medals and...."

"Oh no, Papa," interrupted Laíki, "you've already given two away." He sulked on the floor with the idea of losing another of his favorite things. How could he keep the medals safe if Papa kept using them? Isaac consoled his son but assured him that the family's safety, and even Caliópe's, depended on this.

Besides the medal, Isaac asked Caliópe if he could use the camera she owned. "But George, it has no film," she protested. "It doesn't matter," Isaac countered. He put the camera, the shiny medal and some drachmas on a table near the door.

The beggar returned. Isaac told the family to stay out of sight. The man's stubble of a beard was a bit longer. "Give me some money, please, or you know what will happen." He held his hand out to grasp whatever money would come.

Isaac took the coins and medal in one hand. "Here you are," he offered. "And since you remember me as an athlete, here is a medal I won in Préveza which may be worth something on the black market [illegal market where people could buy things they needed at very expensive prices]."

"And just to make sure you don't come back," Isaac continued as he brought the camera out with his other hand and clicked it, "this photo will be given to the partisans [Resistance Fighters] and you won't see the light of another day."

In the other room, everyone sighed a breath of relief. Laíki was content with only seven gold medals.

The Beggar

Isaac Cohen's medal for broadjumping

THE FOURTH GOLD MEDAL

Wherever the family hid, Laíki still went to school. From Petroúpoli, father and son would take a local bus into Omónia Square and from there, Laíki with his books, would board another bus to go to school.

"Remember Laíki," Isaac began with Laíki interrupting, "meet me here at 4:00 p.m." After a pause both would emphasize with a smile, "Sharp." A hug always ended the instruction.

Even though Isaac went around Athens selling whatever he could find of value, he always managed to be at the bus stop by 4:00 p.m.

This time, no Laíki. What could have happened? Isaac couldn't go to the police. He was afraid someone might see something wrong with his false papers.

An hour passed. A second bus came. No Laíki. Isaac dared not go home. Dora would become fearful and yet the last bus to Petroúpoli left at 6:00 p.m.

Finally, after another hour, Laíki arrived. "Where have you been? What happened?" Isaac scolded the shame-faced boy.

"I'm sorry, Papa, I was playing marbles." His father was already moving Laíki in order to catch the final bus to their hideaway. And on the way, Isaac gave Laíki a spanking, all the time moving him down the street.

Laíki felt the pangs of guilt as well as the pain of his father's hand on his backside. It was a wonder that he still held on to his books.

When the two reached the second bus stop, the station was empty. The bus was gone. "You see what you've done?" Isaac said angrily. "Now we have to walk the four miles home."

Darkness reached Caliópe's house before father and son arrived about 8:00 p.m. Dora waited impatiently by the window. She was angry, yet full of fear as well. Laíki received a second spanking from his mother. "You cannot scare us like that, Pashá," she said when all had quieted down. Laíki understood the difficulty better than ever.

The next morning as Isaac was reading the newspaper he saw an article on page three. "Dora, listen, the bus we missed to Petroúpoli?" Then Isaac read from the article. "All men and boys were taken off the Petroúpoli bus and shot by the Nazis in revenge for the killing of two German officers in downtown Athens."

Tears came to Isaac and Dora's eyes as they realized both he and Laíki would have been lost had they been on that last bus.

Isaac turned to see his son carefully showing the medals to Zoítsa. With a nudge from Dora, Isaac went over and hugged the child. "I'm sorry," he murmured, "we're sorry. If it weren't for your lateness, we would not have come home to your Mama." Laíki hugged him tightly. Zoítsa and Dora joined in. It was a happy, grateful moment, full of tears.

Every few days, Kostas would come by Petroúpoli to say hello to the family and see that all was well. This time, the whole family was there to greet him.

After some small talk with strong Greek coffee at the brightly lit kitchen table, Isaac finally brought up the subject.

"Kostas, I want to leave Greece and go to Palestine where my sister Vicki and her family live. Can you arrange it?" Isaac inquired.

"My friend, it is under British control. Are you sure you'll be able to get through?" Kostas argued.

"We have talked it over," interrupted Dora, "and we think it's the best thing. We have been hiding for months, always afraid of what was next."

Kostas thought a moment. There was nothing he wouldn't do for his friend. "All right," he said sadly, "I'll work out the details and get you some money."

"No, no," Isaac stressed, "we don't need money. I've sold whatever we had at the old apartment and all of my dry goods. But I'm afraid to book passage by boat over to nearby Turkey."

"Is that the way you want to go?" inquired Kostas. "You know you will have to go overland through Syria before you get to Palestine and that route is closely guarded."

"Since I was born in America," Dora answered, "we're hoping the Turkish and Syrian authorities will let us through."

It was true. Dora Cohen had been born in America and since her own family were Greek Jews, they had arranged a marriage between Isaac's family and hers. She married Isaac and stayed in Greece.

Kostas thought it all too risky. Isaac read his thoughts. "My friend," he coaxed, "I love you like a brother and I don't know when I'll see you again but this is what we need to do. Can you get a boat for us?"

Kostas remained silent for a moment looking deeply into Isaac's eyes. "Of course," he said finally.

The family waited anxiously the next few days. By this time, Laíki stopped going to school. Isaac would not tell Caliópe what was happening or where they were going. He was afraid that if she was captured and tortured by the Nazis, it would be best that she knew nothing. It might save her life.

The mailman came to the door. Caliópe opened the door with Isaac not far behind.

"This afternoon at 4:00 p.m. will be a nice time to go out," he said evenly, as he handed the old lady her mail.

"No, no," she responded unknowingly, "that is my nap time." (Greeks are known for their afternoon naps.) But Isaac knew. That was the signal to meet Kostas.

It was decided that Isaac would go alone. The meeting with Kostas was scheduled in Piraéus*, the port city for Athens. There, Isaac would meet the captain of the fishing boat anchored there, the boat that would take him to Évvoia**.

**Piraéus: pronounced "Pi-ray-is"*
***Évvoia: pronounced "Ev-ee-a"*

Map of Greece

It was a complicated plan to get the Cohens out of Greece. First, a small boat would take them from the mainland to the long, thin island of Évvoia. From there, they would cross the island at its thinnest point, to get to the eastern side where a larger boat would carry them on the longer journey into Turkey.

The family waited anxiously at home while Isaac made the long trek from north Athens to Piraéus, which is just south of Greece's largest city.

When Isaac returned, the trio quickly followed him into their room to listen to his instructions. "We will leave in a week. The fisherman told us to meet in Ágia Marína*. He will take us across the water to Évvoia."

Laíki was full of questions. "Where is Ágia Marína? How will we get there? Will we travel at night? What was the captain's name?"

Isaac patiently answered the questions the best he could. "Ágia Marína is near Marathona. Laíki, do you know where the Olympics began?"

Both Laíki and Zoítsa shook their heads.

"Well, they began a long time ago."

In the 1940's, Marathóna was just a beach area east of Athens, but it was famous in ancient times. It was here, 2,500 years ago, that the Greeks defeated the Persians and a runner ran all the way to Athens to tell of the victory. This is where the modern name of 'marathon' for a long distance race comes from.

"So, as you look at the medals you are protecting, Pashá, realize that I too, am part of the athletic tradition that began here in Greece."

** Ágia Marína: pronounced "Ah-ya Ma-reen-a"*

Laíki took his father's face in his little hands. "So, why aren't you in the Olympics? You are the best athlete father in the whole world."

Isaac and Dora laughed and laughed. They needed a good laugh to break the continual tension of not knowing what was coming next. Finally, Isaac said to his proud son, "It is because of you and Zoítsa that I didn't go. I would have had to go to Germany to play. I'd rather live and see you and Zoítsa grow up." A long hug followed.

Laíki's face was beaming, beaming so much that he almost forgot to listen to the answers to his other questions. But Dora took up the second question. "Isaac, how will we get there?"

"There is a bus to Marathóna. From there, there is a local bus to Ágia Marína. But Kostas said we should dress in old clothes as if we are workers or farmers."

"You mean we are dressed too well?" Dora interrupted. They all laughed again because the few clothes they had were well used.

Isaac finished with, "it will take all day for us to get there," knowing how slow busses were and that they might not run on schedule, with the war and all.

They were all ready to leave the room and join Caliópe for dinner when Isaac said to Laíki, "Pashá, the fisherman refused to tell me his name. He is afraid for his family if the Germans find him out. But I know his face, and he is tall as well. We'll find him when we get to Ágia Marína."

Caliópe knew something was brewing when the family became so quiet at dinner. But she never asked questions. And Laíki ate his stuffed tomato thinking he would enjoy Caliópe's cooking at least one more week.

The week passed slowly. Each member of the family had his or her ideas and images about the upcoming trip of their lives. Isaac kept going over the details of the trip to Évvoia; Dora feared the unknown; Laíki wondered if he could keep the medals safe; and Zoítsa, well, at her age she didn't think about it much at all.

Every morning Calióре would go to the local market to see what few vegetables she could buy. With the German occupation, the Nazis would get first choice. There was very little left for the Greeks. When Isaac said, "Don't worry about buying too much for us, Calióре," she knew that on this day she may not see the family again. And for the family, it was the best time to leave.

It was Saturday, and although it was the Jewish Sabbath (the Jews usually go to Synagogue and pray on Saturday), it would be a good day to travel because no one would expect Jewish people to travel on what was a holy day.

After Calióре left with her empty shopping bag, the family dressed to leave. They looked fatter than usual but with no baggage. Everyone had layers of clothing on. They could not carry any luggage because they could not let anyone know that they were trying to leave the country.

Isaac carried the money needed; Dora, her American passport, some cheese and nuts; and Laíki, the seven medals. Zoítsa just held Mama's hand.

Laíki knew by now that one of the seven medals would remain behind. And he asked his father if he could put it somewhere special. "Where do you think, Pashá?"

"In the kitchen," Laíki responded, "because it always smells so good." Isaac laughed in agreement and lifted the little boy up so that the medal could be put in one of the cupboards, right near the olive oil, that was also so precious during this time of war.

THE FIFTH GOLD MEDAL

The bus from Petroúpoli took the four members of the Cohen family to Omónia Square. Laíki was familiar with this part of the trip. Although it was January and cold, the sun was shining. The extra clothes helped keep the family warm.

The bus to Marathóna was about a mile away, yet close to the hospital where Kostas worked as a doctor and where he hid other Jews under beds and as patients. Isaac needed to say goodbye to his life-long friend.

"Isaac," Dora protested as they walked towards the second bus, "it is so dangerous. You know the German army has their headquarters right across the street from the hospital."

"Yes, I do know," Isaac said quietly, "but how can I leave without saying goodbye to my brother? After all he's done for us?"

"It's just that I am more fearful when we are separated, Isaac. We have a long day ahead of us, and it tires me just to think of anything extra."

Isaac put his arm around her. "It will only take a moment." He turned to Laíki. "Pashá, when we come to the hospital, I will need another medal." Laíki understood far better than his age. He loved the Good Doctor almost as much as his father did.

Quietly, as they were walking, Laíki secretly took one of the medals out of the bag, one with a blue and white ribbon still attached, and gave it to his father as he took Isaac's hand. No one saw the transfer. In a few minutes, Isaac put it in his own coat pocket.

Laíki knew the next part also. In the few times he and his father went to visit Kostas at the hospital, Laíki would always play sick with a stomach ache and Isaac would ask for Dr. Nikoláou to look at the 'terrible problem' Laíki had.

Anna, Kostas' wife and a volunteer nurse at the hospital, was usually at the front desk. When she wasn't working at the hospital, she dressed as a nurse and would take free food to the nearby old age home, hoping that no bombs or bullets would find her while she went about Athens. She thought that the nurse's uniform would help keep her safe.

This day, she was at the front desk and she, too, knew the ritual.

The double front doors opened into a long, wide hallway with Anna's desk on the left. With Dora and Zoítsa sitting and waiting on the front steps, Isaac carrying a 'sick' Laíki entered. Anna smiled at them knowingly but before she could greet them, a commotion broke out at the end of the hall.

It was Kostas and a German soldier with a rifle. Kostas was yelling and screaming as he came running towards Isaac.

"What are you doing here, again? Didn't I tell you yesterday not to come back? You beggars are all the same!"

The medal with ribbon attached

Kostas turned to the soldier even though he was moving towards Isaac. "These beggars, they have no home!" He motioned to the soldier with one finger indicating "just one minute."

He quickly grabbed a stunned Isaac and Laíki. "Go on, get out," he said loudly, turning them towards the door. In a whisper, he said in Isaac's ear, "The Germans are searching for Jews. They're going through the whole hospital. I'm trying to stall them." Isaac understood.

And loudly again he continued, "What? The child's stomach again?" With his back to the soldier Kostas quickly opened Laíki's jacket and whispered "something for your trip." He quickly put a soft package into the little boy's jacket and closed the garment again. Then continuing loudly, "It's nothing. He won't feel better until the war is over. Now, get out of here and don't come back. Here's the door."

As Kostas pushed the duo out, Isaac reached into Kostas' smock and put the medal securely into the large pocket.

"Oh, and this must be your wife and other child. Well, get out of here, all of you! Leave us alone. I don't want to see you until the war is over!" And in a last whisper, "Isaac, your brother Jacob will meet you there."

Kostas slammed the door shut and motioned with his body to the soldier at the far end, as if saying, "What are you going to do?" He winked at Anna as he passed her, proceeding towards the German soldiers who were now gathering at the end of the hall...empty handed.

Kostas smiled as he put his hands in his smock's pockets. It slowed him down a bit as he massaged the medal and ribbon that he found. He knew. Isaac was Greece's best athlete. He saw the medals many times. Kostas smiled for both reasons. The Cohens were on their way and the soldiers found no Jews.

Outside, Laíki wondered if the Doctor still loved him as he used to. Isaac calmed him as he related the story to Dora. They walked towards the bus stop. The Marathóna bus happened to be on time. They climbed aboard, taking seats, already exhausted.

But Isaac couldn't rest. Where was Jacob to meet the family? At Ágia Marína? How was he to get there? Did he know what time? But little by little, Isaac, and the rest of the family, fell asleep.

There was little to worry about for the moment. They were leaving the heavily patrolled downtown of Athens, and Marathóna was the last stop for this bus.

The long bus ride was full of naps, eating the little bit of food the family had, thinking of Jacob and finding the package that the Good Doctor gave to Laíki. It was full of medical supplies for the trip to Turkey with a small, unsigned note: "Do not forget us." Tears came to Isaac's eyes because he truly thought that he might never see his childhood friend again.

The brakes on the old bus screeched as it came to a stop and the driver announced loudly that it was Marathóna. It woke the four up with a start. They quickly mingled with the other passengers getting off the bus. Now, the problem was to find the bus to Ágia Marína.

Marathóna was not a big city. The downtown was closing for the afternoon siesta. Very few stores were open. Isaac went into a grocery story that was still open and asked for directions. The woman behind the counter didn't know if there was a bus to the port town.

Outside Laíki caught sight of an old man loading his wagon with goods. Laíki had never seen many horses before so he moved closer to get a better look.

"Laíki, come back," his mother warned.

"It's alright, lady," the old robust man called back. "The horse is very friendly."

Dora was torn between waiting for Isaac and moving towards Laíki. She lifted Zoítsa into her arms and moved towards the horse and wagon all the while looking over her shoulder.

"Want to pet him?" the smiling farmer asked Laíki.

"Can I, Mama?" Laíki asked turning to Dora.

"Alright, alright, but be careful," she cautioned. She took a long look at the grocery store.

"Mama, Mama, look at me," Laíki giggled. When Dora quickly turned back, the boy was in the driver's seat.

"Laíki, you come down right now!"

"Lady, it is all right. Where are you from? By the way you're dressed I can tell you're not from Marathóna," the farmer said warmly.

"Athens," Dora said curtly. In the meantime, Isaac had come out of the store, found where the family moved to and ran over.

"Good afternoon," the old man said to Isaac as Isaac stopped short behind Dora. "You have a good little boy here and what eyes. Just like my grandson. Mister, where is your family headed?"

Isaac and Dora had the same thought as they glanced at each other. "Ágia Marína," Isaac finally said. "This farmer looked safe," Isaac thought.

"Ooohhh, I live right outside Ágia Marína. Do you want a ride?"

"Yes!" Laíki shouted.

Dora protested, "We were waiting for a bus...."

"What bus?" the farmer laughed. "Sometimes it runs, most times it doesn't. So come, I'll take you over." He climbed onto the seat next to Laíki. "Jump in the back. We'll get you there in a half hour or so."

"Can I stay up here, Mama?" pleaded Laíki.

"Of course you can," interrupted the owner. "I need help driving the wagon."

"Oh boy!" responded Laíki enthusiastically.

"Be careful with what you're carrying, Pashá," Isaac warned his child as the other three climbed into the back. Laíki put his hand on his inner shirt. The medals were still safe and the road to the waterside was waiting for an assistant driver!

The ride to Ágia Marína was a bumpy one. Some of the bombings had ripped up parts of the road. But it was a happy moment for Laíki when the old man handed the reins to him so that he could lead the horse. But the horse knew the way home. He had done it often.

"There is a bag with kouloúria* (plural for a round bread shaped like a bagel covered with sesame seeds)," shouted the old man from up front. "Have some." It was as if the old man knew the situation but if he did, he didn't let on.

When it was time to continue on their journey, the old man congratulated Laíki for his superb driving with a kouloúri of his own.

**kouloúria – pronounced "kou-<u>lou</u>-ree-a"*

"Where is the paralía* (the water front)," Isaac asked as he graciously thanked the farmer. The farmer pointed, "It is straight down at the bottom of this road."

The day was almost over as the family proceeded a few hundred yards to the waterfront. Ágia Marína was such a small town that there was only one kafenío** (coffee shop) and as the quartet walked in, there was the fisherman sitting at one of the tables. He motioned them over to come and sit. Only when the sun went down would they start the next part of their journey.

The fisherman was the captain of his own boat. He was a foreigner from Hungary who escaped from his country just before the Nazis attacked and overtook it. He came to Greece thinking it was safer only to find the same situation had overcome this country as well. He spoke rarely because of his heavy Hungarian accent. He was afraid the Germans might find him out and send his whole family back. Or worse, kill them all.

Isaac found out that the man still refused to give his name, but did not refuse to take the agreed upon amount of money – 320 drachmés***. He was a poor fisherman in his native country as well. It was easy to pick up the same work here in Greece. "I'm sorry but the family needs this," he said earnestly. Isaac understood.

It was time. Darkness had finally come. When they all stood to leave, Laíki noticed how tall this man was, taller than his father. They walked slowly to the dock where the boat was

** paralía – pronounced "pa-ra-<u>lee</u>-a"*
***kafenío – pronounced "kaf-en-<u>ee</u>-o"*
****drachmés – pronounced "drak-<u>mes</u>": Greek money; in 1943, 320 drachmés was approximately $80 of American money.*

moored. It was so small. “How can we all fit on it?” thought Laíki. “And how can he fit on it? He’s so tall.”

But fit they did, and although it was cramped, it was only about an hour to the western shore of Évvoia, the island they needed to get to.

The fisherman never got out of the boat and hurriedly started back after the group of four got out. Isaac looked around. There was not much to see on this beach. The town looked small up on the hill. There were rocks and bushes at various spots along the seashore.

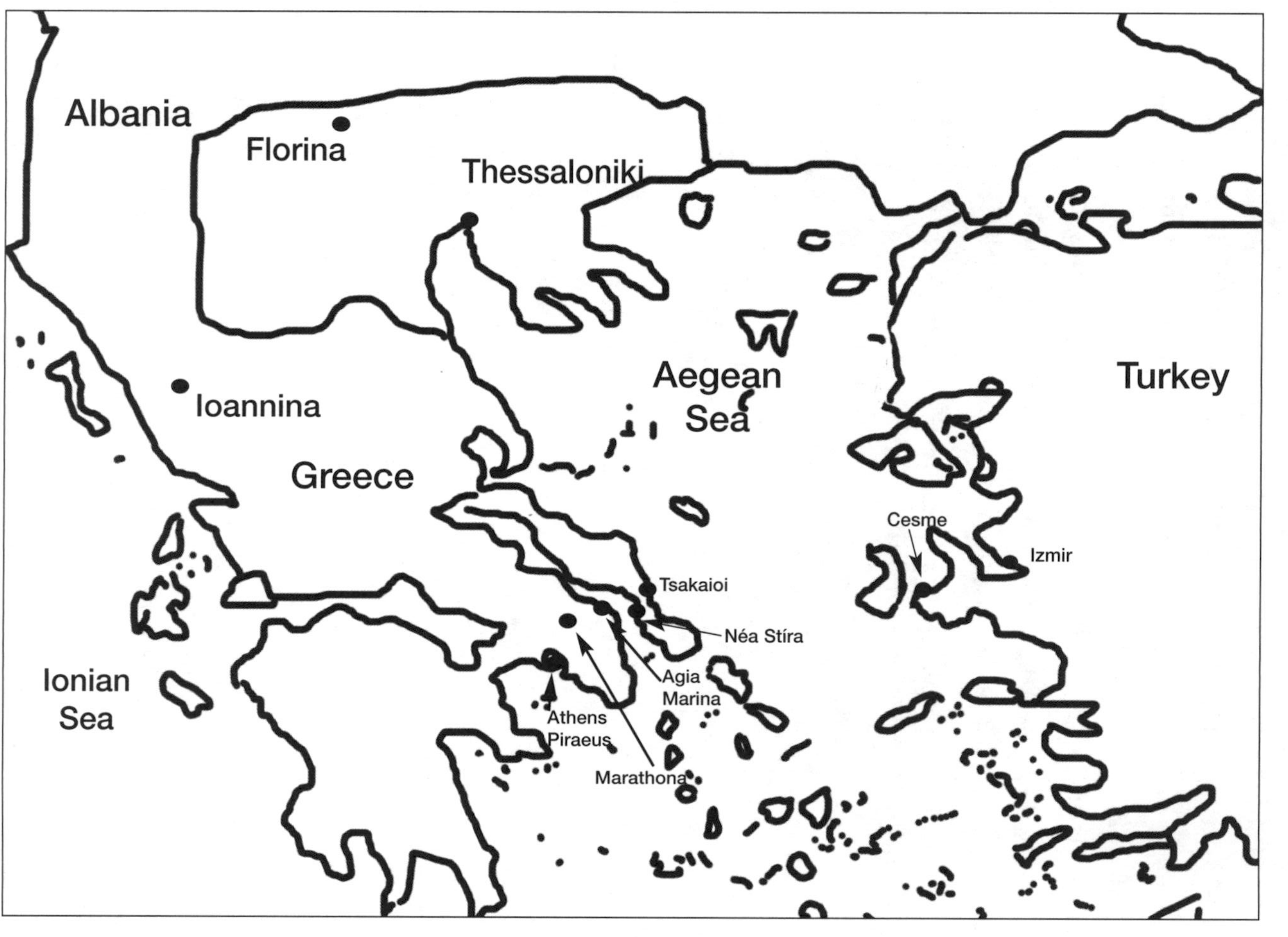

Escape from Greece

THE SIXTH GOLD MEDAL

The wind was picking up as the family made their way up the beach. Behind rocks and bushes came a commanding voice, "Who is it and what do you want?" It stopped everyone in their tracks.

"I am George Hellás," Isaac shouted," and this is my family." He waited.

"Who sent you?" came the voice.

"Kostas Nikoláou, the doctor," Isaac called back.

Dora whispered, "Maybe we're in the wrong place."

Isaac hushed her and waited.

The bushes rattled and over a rock came this lean mustached man in crumpled clothing. He carried a rifle and a holstered gun. "Very good," he said. "So you're the athlete that Kostas talks about. You're a bit early, but so are the others. Come join them."

He led the Cohen family behind some large rocks and there were huddled five other people anxious to leave Greece. Isaac assumed there would be more people, and he started looking for his brother, Jacob, but easily saw that he wasn't among the other escapees. As they settled in with the small group of newcomers, Laíki wanted to know where they were. One of the strangers told him before Isaac could ask the same question. It was Néa Stíra*.

"In a little while," the leader began, "one of our comrades is bringing as many donkeys as he can find. We will travel through the night to reach Tsakaíoi**, on the other side of the island. It is a slow journey over some hills before we reach the eastern side."

He looked around. He saw that there were nine people. All together there were two women, two children, and the rest young men. "The women and children will ride. The rest of us walk. If there are enough donkeys, others may switch back and forth."

"What about the Germans?" a man asked, worriedly.

The leader turned to him, a little taken aback. "You are safe here with us. The Germans do not chance coming up here out of the city. They know it's dangerous for them, especially at night. And we are very cautious."

He waited for any other questions. There weren't any. The leader looked at the children and smiled. Everything would be all right. All they had to do is wait. The leader said no more.

Zoítsa fell asleep in Mama's arms. Laíki sat near Isaac to gain some warmth from the wind that had picked up. It began to rain.

**Néa Stíra: pronounced "Nay-a Stih-ra"*

*** Tsakaíoi: pronounced "Tsa-kay-ee"*

The only sounds now were the wind and the soft rain. The people were silent, waiting. After some time, they heard some hoof beats. It was the donkeys. There were only two with one man leading them.

The leader went up to meet him. "Don't worry," the runaways could hear him say, "you'll get them back tomorrow."

After the anxious waiting, the people were ready to leave no matter how long or short a time it was. Dora got on one donkey, carrying a sleeping Zoítsa. The other woman got on the other donkey. Laíki chose to walk with his father.

As they were loading, Isaac moved towards the silent leader and asked, "Were we expecting anyone else? My brother was supposed to meet us."

"Maybe in Tsakaíoi," was his abrupt answer. Nothing more needed to be said. Only the rain and wind continued their conversation.

The troupe of people started off the beach. They had a full night ahead of them and the rain wasn't letting up. Everyone was miserable, especially Dora who started to sob silently.

Isaac and Laíki came close to the donkey. "Dora, what's the matter?" Isaac asked the agitated woman. Dora just sobbed and her tears mixed with the rain. Zoítsa awakened and also started to sob.

The leader turned from the front position but said nothing.

"Dora, please, a little while longer," Isaac said comforting his wife. "Soon, we will be with our family in Tel Aviv. A little longer." He took Zoítsa from Dora and held her in his arms to quiet her. The leader motioned to Laíki to come up to him and walk alongside. Although the mud slowed him a bit, Laíki ran toward the opportunity.

The road ahead looked dark. Suddenly lights flickered on at a farmhouse. "Our first and only stop," the leader whispered loudly. Everyone was relieved. A little bit of rest was needed by everyone, especially Dora.

The group clamored into the old farmhouse. The small, thin farmer and his wife had readied some coffee and sweets, all this in the middle of the night. The owners greeted the leader like an old friend with hugs and kisses. They were all working to free Greece as they helped Jews escape the jaws of death.

Everyone slumped in chairs around a long table. The fireplace was lit with warmth and the husband and wife served everyone as if they were royalty. Well, Isaac's new name represented 'George, the King,' anyway. They even had a bathroom to wash up in!

As the husband came to Isaac with his coffee, Isaac asked, "What is this man's name, the one who leads us? He didn't tell us."

"He never does. We only know him by his code name: Avierinós*. He is the commander of Greek Resistance in this area."

Isaac repeated the name to himself a few times to commit it to memory.

Dora, meanwhile, had slumped on the table, alternately napping and sobbing when she awakened every few minutes.

The leader, Avierinós, gave the group some extra time to dry off as best they could, with hopes that the rain would let up. It would be easier going if it did.

** Avierinós: pronounced "Av-yer-ee-nos"; means 'morning star'; his real name was Vasílis Perseídis [Per-say-dis]*

Avierinós

Isaac huddled with his family. Zoítsa was still drowsy but Isaac needed to know if Dora could go on. "Don't ask me, now. It is a bad time to decide." The warmth and dryness calmed Dora down. Outside light was upon the weary group even though the sun wasn't up yet.

"The boat to take you to Turkey," began Avierinós, "is due tonight. We still have a few hours ahead of us. Once we get to Tsakaíoi, we will disperse. Go to a kafenío, sit in the park, go sightseeing, walk along the paralía, and we'll meet again this evening after dark on the beach."

"Mama, are you alright?" Laíki asked Dora, worried that they might turn back. Dora took a good look at her son with the big, bright eyes. Could she ever forgive herself if they went back and something happened to the boy? There wasn't much of a future for the family under Nazi rule. She understood that freedom meant more than how she felt at any given moment.

She took Laíki's face, kissed it on both cheeks, hugged him, and rocked him. "Yes, Pashá, yes, I am alright."

The trek began anew. The day was coming up. The rain had become a drizzle. The wind became a breeze for the moment. Was the worst over? Jacob seemed to be the biggest question now. And since he was talked about enough, Laíki worried a bit about his favorite uncle.

In a few hours, they knew they were near Tsakaíoi because of the bells. It was Sunday and every town in Greece has a church because religion is such a strong part of everyone's life. All work stopped on Sunday. People relaxed as best they could under these conditions of war. It was easier for the Cohens to mingle with the townspeople. And everywhere they went, Isaac would take a quick look to see if Jacob had arrived. No luck.

The breeze was the only thing that followed the family overnight. Sometimes it became a gust of wind but for a Sunday in January, it was milder than normal.

Finally, evening came and under the cover of darkness, about 25 individuals became a large group on the beach. And the wind joined them as they settled in for another wait. The family walked amidst the new faces searching for the familiar face of Jacob.

Laíki spied his uncle first. “There he is,” he exclaimed as he ran to his uncle for a kiss and a lift. Zoítsa followed.

Isaac saw that Jacob had lost weight since he had last seen him. Everyone was starving. “You look good, brother,” Isaac fibbed. Jacob returned the gesture along with a hug and two kisses.

“Where did you go today? How come we didn’t see you?” Isaac asked, happy to see his younger brother.

“I went to church,” Jacob said with a straight face. This, coming from a man who hardly went to synagogue. “And after services were over I told the priest that I could help him clean up. I am a very slow worker, so I was there all day. Did you bring the money for my fare?” Jacob continued trying not to be too anxious.

“Don’t worry,” Isaac scolded him, as he pinched his brother’s two cheeks and tapped them as he always did.

As they sat down in the sand, Isaac noticed no other children as young as Laíki and Zoítsa. Laíki noticed it also and huddled close to his Uncle Jacob for warmth, as the wind was picking up once again.

Avierinós also arrived. As 'Captain' of the resistance here, he wanted to make sure things ran smoothly.

Every little while he would make his rounds of the people. When he came to the Cohen family, he asked Isaac to walk with him along the beach while waiting for the boat. "I want to hear about your medals," he said jokingly.

The wind was still kicking as the Captain began his lecture. "Listen, if the wind is this high here at the beach, there is probably a storm on the sea itself. I don't think you should let the children go. The boat may not make it across."

"But I can't leave them here," Isaac protested loudly overcoming the whipping wind.

"I'm just warning you, but you can't tell the others. If you do, I'll call you a liar, understand?"

Isaac nodded. "So tell me about how you won the medals," the Captain laughed. "It's good to be in such a famous person's company."

As they walked back, Isaac briefly told him how he had won the medals. His most famous medal was the one for javelin. He had thrown the javelin well beyond where the farthest spectator was sitting. Isaac also told him how he was the flag-holder for the discus team. But, most of all he told him how fast he could run, beating all the others in the Épirus* county area. Épirus was the part of Greece where he was born. Préveza was one of the cities in the area.

When Isaac got back to his family, he sat his chilled body down silently to wait. Laíki watched as his father did not say a word until the boat came.

** Épirus: pronounced: "Ee-pi-rus"*

The waiting crowd rose as one with excitement as the boat came into view. Isaac noticed that the wind was still blowing strong.

The boat shut its motor as it came closer to the shore. A sailor jumped into the icy water and brought the towline so that the small craft could be pulled to the beach. It would be a few wet steps for the Jews to be on their way to freedom.

Isaac stopped the family in its tracks. "I'm not going," he announced. The crowd grumbled.

"What are you saying, Isa...George?" Dora blurted out.

"We are not going," Isaac reiterated.

Now the crowd was getting angry. "Is there something wrong with the boat? Are you a spy? Are you a Nazi? Do you know something we don't know?" The uproar took the captain of the boat by surprise. He quickly jumped into the water and came up to the group.

"What's going on here?" he said in a deep heavy voice. He was from the island of Cyprus. He looked well-fed compared to the others. The money he made from this secretive and dangerous work allowed him to eat well.

"My family and I have decided not to go." Isaac stood firm. "But why?" Dora clamored. "You brought us here, this close to freedom, and now you say 'no'? "Think of your children!"

"I am," countered Isaac.

Suddenly someone in the crowd took out a gun and pointed it right at Isaac. "Tell us!" he shouted.

The captain tried to calm everyone down. "If all of you don't go, I lose a lot of money."

"I'm not going," Isaac continued. He was not going to give in.

"Something must be wrong with the boat. Is that it?" the man holding the gun continued. "So you and your family and your brother will be safe here while we risk our lives for you. Is that it?" The man with the gun clicked the hammer open.

"I don't know anything," Isaac insisted. "And neither do I," Jacob interrupted. "I trust what my brother is saying so I will go with you. You'll be assured he wouldn't leave me in any danger."

They all looked at Isaac. Isaac's face showed no emotion. He dug deep into his pocket and gave the money for his brother's passage, and then turned to Laíki for another one of the gold medals.

"I know you have no money," Isaac said to Jacob. "Maybe this will help when you need to pay for something."

As the anger subsided, all made their way onto the boat, Jacob waving a last goodbye. The beach was empty now except for the Cohens, Captain Avierinós and four gold medals nestled close to Laíki 's sleepy body.

THE SEVENTH GOLD MEDAL

Before long, the sound of the boat was gone, but its light could still be faintly seen. The wind still blew strongly. "Come," said Avierinós to the chilled family, "let's find you some lodging and food."

They walked up the hill to the town where everyone was already asleep and the shutters of houses drawn closed.

"This man, here, is a banker. You can stay over till the next boat comes." The Captain knocked on the door a few times before the banker appeared.

The man was half-awake in his nightclothes as the group tramped in. "I want you to take care of these Jews, until the next boat comes to pick up another group," Avierinós barked.

"But Captain, what if the children say something. I have kids of my own. I am a respectable citizen of Tsakaíoi. I need to be careful. I deal with the Germans everyday...."

"You will put these people in your beds and you will sleep on the floor," ordered the Resistance leader. "And you will feed them before you eat. Is that understood?" The red-faced banker nodded his head in agreement.

Isaac interrupted. "Please, I don't want to stay here where we're not wanted. There must be another house."

The Captain eyed the banker as he let him off the hook. "Yes, there is. I'll take you there. But I'll remember this the next time we have to cross paths, Mr. Banker!" he said as he spat out his last words.

Yiánni and Popi welcomed their guests just as Captain Avierinós would have wanted. Yiánni was a schoolteacher and Popi worked in the local government office. They had children of their own, Leonídas and Viví, short for Victoria, and for the next few days a peace came over the Cohen family.

The children played together and there was no problem with religion getting in the way. On Sunday, they all went to church, the Cohens pretending that they were long lost cousins and Zoítsa learning to make the sign of the cross.

The Cohen family knew that a boat would be arriving soon because strangers started gathering the day after church. As evening grew, the crowd grew and Isaac, Dora and the two children joined them.

The only thing they left behind as a memento for the family in Tsakaíoi was one of Isaac's medals. Laíki now had three to keep safe.

THE LAST OF THE GOLD MEDALS

Laíki knew that before he got on the boat, he would probably only have two shiny medals. And he was right.

On this clear, cold evening, there was no wind and all was well.

"Well, George, Mr. Athlete," Captain Avierinós was saying, "I know you will have a safer journey now. I know the captain of this boat. He's a Frenchman. He'll get you there in one piece."

Amid the hugs and kisses, Isaac slipped a medal into the leader's pocket. Laíki saw this and smiled.

As they boarded the boat, one captain shouted to the other, "This is a great Greek athlete. Treat him well!" The Frenchman nodded as Isaac gave him money for the four of them.

"How do I know how great he is?" the boat captain shouted back. "He's won gold medals for his work," bellowed Avierinós. "Let him show you."

Laíki obediently took out the two gold medals that were left. The Frenchman looked at them closely. "I'll take them," he said quickly with a smile.

"But Papa," Laíki protested. Isaac tried to quiet the boy as the child cried against his father's body. "It's all right, Pashá, we still have each other."

That didn't help Laíki at all. All he had was an empty bag to hold on to. And Zoítsa's hand as she grabbed Laíki's to hold on to.

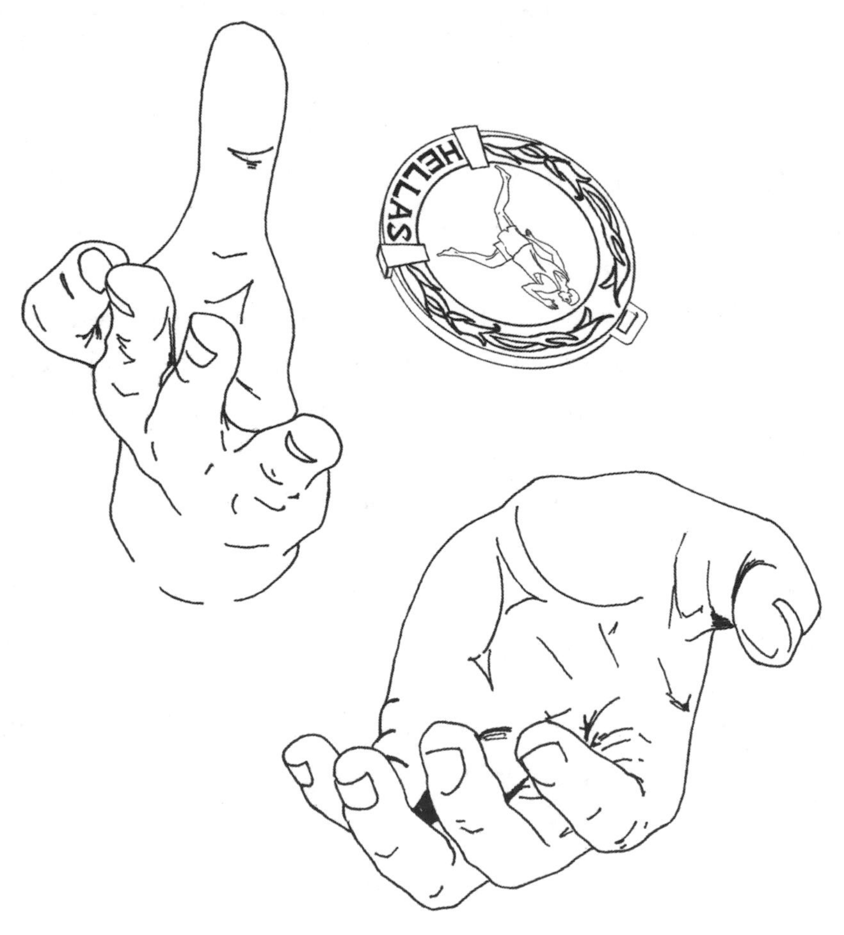

The Last Of the Medals

The small boat was full of fish and people. The family found a spot in the bottom of the boat where the fish were stored. It was wet and dingy. Twenty-seven other Jews went into the belly of this overloaded craft. Laíki and Zoítsa sat between Dora and Isaac.

The motor revved and slowly they were off. Even in calm weather the coldness of the winter swept right through the small boat. There was no light, no talk, no movement except for the rocking and creaking of the boat. The waves splashed against the craft continuously.

"Papa, my legs, I cannot feel them," Laíki blurted out. "I cannot feel them!" "Shhhh, it's all right, Pashá," Isaac calmed his son. "Lay them over my legs and I'll rub them until they are alive again," he chuckled.

The seven or eight hours seemed like forever to the children. Zoítsa finally fell asleep in Dora's arms. Laíki's big eyes were wide with fear.

Gunfire erupted with the morning sun. If Laíki's eyes closed at any time during the long night, they were wide open now. The commotion awakened everyone in the underbelly of the boat.

Suddenly the boat rocked with a hit to one side. "What is happening, Papa?" Laíki cried. Zoítsa cried without words. Dora and Isaac held the children close.

"Don't worry," they heard the captain shouting down. "Don't worry. We will still make it to Turkish waters. Stay quiet. Those rotten Nazis!" he added.

To stop the attack, the French captain put up a white flag but did not stop the boat. It put-putted into the Turkish area. The German boat was catching up, but did not fire another round.

The shore was near. "Halt!" the German captain shouted through a loud speaker as their boat drew near. "Stop right now!"

"I cannot shut the motor," the Frenchman responded as loud as he could.

Other boats from the shoreline could be seen coming. By the time the German boat pulled along side, so did the two Turkish patrol boats.

The stowaways heard all of this in total silence. Laíki and Zoítsa's mouths were covered with their parents' hands.

As soon as the Turkish boats came, the Germans departed with a curt, "Sorry." They didn't want to offend a country that might enter the war on their side. Turkey was neutral. They were trying to stay out of the war, but thirty years ago, during World War I, Turkey had joined the German side. The Germans were hoping they would still do that in this war. The Germans had to be careful not to upset the Turks.

Slowly the fishing boat was escorted into the port of Césme*. The Jews breathed easier. Safety was at hand.

The boat's motor finally gave out. The Jews needed to tramp through water once again to get to dry land and safety. Laíki and Zoítsa were carried by their parents. The air smelled so clean, so fresh, so free.

"Isaac, wait a minute. Wait," called Dora who was a little behind some of the other people. "I lost one of my shoes in the water."

Isaac came back with the older child to search. Under the watchful eye of the Turkish authorities, they looked to see if the shoe would wash up onto the shore. No such luck.

Laíki thought Mama walked like a bunny rabbit with just one shoe on.

**Césme: pronounced "Chez-meh"*

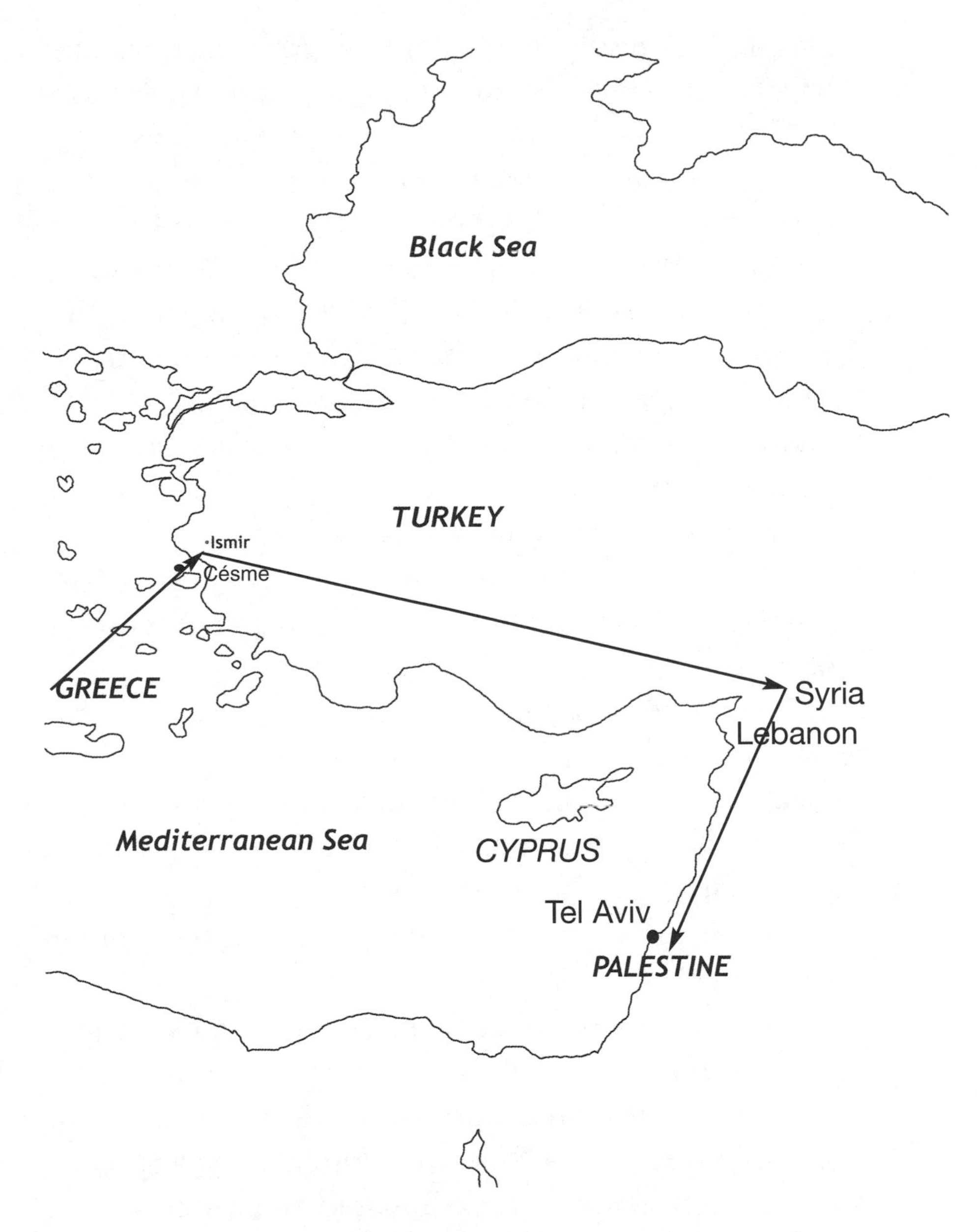

Route from Greece to Turkey to Palestine

When the four finally entered the dingy room where the other Jews were being questioned, Dora was still missing a shoe. But Dora still had her American passport securely in her possession. That was more important.

When it was their turn to come to the desk to be interviewed, the American passport worked wonders. The Turkish officer looked them over quickly, asked a few questions and told them where they could find an American representative in Izmír*, the city closest to Césme, where they landed.

"We have no money to get there," Dora protested. The Turkish officer gave them bus fare, a little extra for food and an official note just in case anyone stopped them.

Dora decided to take the other shoe off since it was easier to walk barefoot. Laíki decided that it was a great way to fill his empty, colorful bag.

Izmír was one of the largest cities in Turkey. It took awhile to find the American embassy. After waiting an hour in the front room, Dora was asked to come alone into the inner office. There, a tall, lean man wearing a suit and tie with glasses on his long, thin face asked her to sit down.

"Mrs. Cohen, I see by your passport that you were born in America. Where?"

"New York," she answered, hoping this would be short. The children were hungry.

Over the red-covered passport, the clerk eyed her. He saw a person with no shoes and rumpled clothing. She was wearing clothing upon clothing. He compared the photo on the passport with her appearance. Could she be one and the same? Could she be an American?

**Izmír: pronounced "Iz-meer"*

"Uhh, Mrs. Cohen," he continued, "it would be best if I wire Washington, DC to see what I'm to do next." Dora started to worry. "Come back in a week or two and we'll have an answer," he concluded in a gruff voice.

Before the man could stand up to say goodbye, Dora began. "You want me to come back in a week or two? I have two starving children out there. And a husband who has done everything to bring us to safety. I have one shoe!" she clamored as she quickly opened the door she came through, grabbed Laíki's colorful bag and ran back into the office. "You want me to wait two weeks?" she yelled as she showed him the shoe and threw it on his desk. "What is the passport good for?"

Laíki was just as surprised as everyone else in the office. Both children drew closer to their father. "Don't worry, your mother will handle it," he whispered in Greek.

"Do you want to ask me questions? Ask me questions," Dora berated the stunned official. "My father's name is Isaac Albala. My mother's maiden name is Anna Dostis. I have three brothers, all in America — Nathan, Benny and Morris."

She was a roller coaster now. "After my father died, my mother couldn't take care of all of us, so my brother Morris and I were put into a home for children. What else do you want to know?"

"All this was personal," thought the clerk. "How many baseball teams does New York have?" he asked trying to catch her. "The Yankees in the American League and the Dodgers and Giants in the National League," countered Dora easily.

That did it. The clerk signed an order to give the Cohens money for food, transportation and another pair of shoes for Dora. Laíki, Zoítsa and Isaac saw a beaming Dora come out of the office. “ Laíki,” she whispered, “we won’t need the other shoe. I’m getting new ones!”

The trip south towards Tel-Aviv where the rest of Isaac’s family lived was, indeed, easier. Except for delays with trains and busses, the only thing Isaac and the family needed to be careful about now was not to speak Greek. Since Palestine [now Israel] was under British control, they were afraid that speaking Greek would get them sent to a detention camp on Cyprus, which was also under British control.

Dora spoke English, Isaac spoke French. Either of those languages would do. “Listen to me closely children,” Isaac began the instruction. “You cannot talk when other people are around. Do you understand?”

“But why?” Zoítsa asked. “Because people around here might send us to jail, Koukla,” responded Dora using the affectionate Greek term for ‘doll.’ The children understood and nodded in agreement.

The family proceeded through Turkey, and since France controlled Syria, the French language got the family through that country to British controlled Palestine. With the children obeying their parents and Isaac not saying a word, Dora’s passport did most of the talking.

Finding Vicki, her husband Pepo, and their daughters, Joya and Neomi in Tel Aviv was a most happy occasion. Hugs and kisses, and warm looks continued for days.

“So, where is Jacob?” Isaac asked innocently. “I want to see my brother.”

“Jacob?” Vicki asked. “We haven’t heard from him in months. He was in Greece with you.” Isaac kept his thoughts to himself. He looked over at Dora. She caught his eye and they both knew that something might have gone wrong since he left many days before the rest of the family.

Laíki also thought it funny that Uncle Jacob wasn't there yet but it was only a passing thought. He now could play in the open with his cousins. He had clean clothes. He ate when he wanted. He slept in a bed. What more could he ask for?

It was morning and Laíki in his half sleep could hear footsteps running towards his Aunt Vicki's apartment above the fabric store where they lived.

"Vicki, Vicki," was the urgent call. Laíki peeked out of the window. It was his Uncle Pepo, Vicki's husband. The slim but muscular man should have been at the docks working.

"Laíki, Laíki," he yelled as he saw Laíki's face, "get your Aunt down here quickly." Laíki ran to the other room. "Aunt Vicki, Aunt Vicki," he said as he rushed to her bedside, "Uncle Pepo wants you downstairs, now."

"Why? What's happening?" she wondered out loud as she put on a robe. "I don't know, but he's yelling for you," Laíki cried out in excitement.

As his aunt ran downstairs, so did his father. Dora gathered the children as everyone in the household was up.

Laíki ran to his window once again. He could see the emotions of the three downstairs, and Uncle Pepo pointing to his window, but he couldn't make out what they were saying.

Just as quickly, Pepo, on the run, departed and Vicki and her brother Isaac came inside.

Laíki wondered what could be so important.

"What's happening?" Dora asked Isaac as he came into the room. "It's Jacob. He's been caught." Isaac began dressing. "He's in the prison in Gaza waiting to be taken to the large

British prison on the island of Cyprus." Gaza was a city in an area in Palestine also controlled by the British. Uncle Jacob was in great danger.

"What are you going to do?" Dora asked.

"Pepo knows someone with a car. We need to get a pass from the British to get in. Hopefully, we'll get Jacob out before the next boat leaves for Cyprus," Isaac replied.

He knelt down to Laíki. "Uncle Pepo thinks that if you come along, the guards will not become suspicious and we have a better chance to get Uncle Jacob out. You can identify him. What do you think?"

Laíki quickly looked at his mother to see what her reaction would be. "Isn't that dangerous, Isaac?" Dora cautioned.

"Yes," Isaac responded softly still looking at Laíki. "Uncle Jacob is also in a dangerous position. A Mr. Mamoúd will take you inside the prison so that you can point Uncle Jacob out."

"Why not you or Pepo?" Dora argued. Isaac looked at her. "Both of us are Greeks. Laíki, if he does it silently, will not arouse suspicions. Are you willing Pashá?" Isaac softly whispered to Laíki.

"Can I, Mama?"

Dora was anxious but she understood how important this was. She nudged Laíki to say yes. "Alright...good," Isaac beamed as he rose up. Dora moved towards her husband while Laíki dashed over to his bed to get dressed. "Please be very careful," she whispered lovingly, with a hug.

The embrace was long enough for Laíki to run out of the room and down the stairs. "Remember not to say a word," Dora yelled after the boy.

Pepo's friend Mamoúd worked on the docks also, loading and unloading boats. He, too, was muscular and of an Egyptian family who settled in the port city. And he owned a car.

It took less than a couple of hours to go from Tel Aviv to the Gaza jail where Jacob Cohen was held. Since Mamoúd spoke English well, he might not have a problem visiting. And, if anyone asked, Laíki was his nephew.

They parked the vehicle at the far end of the open compound that was surrounded by a fence topped with barbed wire. They kept the motor running.

Tents and low buildings filled this huge prison. The problem was that Mamoúd didn't know what Jacob looked like. This is where Laíki came in.

Mamoúd walked from the car to the front gate with the small boy and a small bag of food. There was already a long line of visitors waiting to get in. The sun was beginning to heat up the day. But it wasn't the heat that made Laíki sweat. He was afraid and excited at the same time.

The British guards went through the lines quickly looking at whatever parcels people had and giving them a stamped slip of paper so that the same person could get out of the prison when the visit was over.

With a curt exchange of hellos, Mamoúd received his dated piece of paper with 'boy' added to it and walked in with his bag of food. Now, to find Laíki's uncle.

Laíki kept silent as he was told to do. As both man and boy walked through the prisoners, Laíki's eyes glanced here and there. All at once Jacob's face came out from behind a crowd. Jacob was ready to say something when Laíki shook his head "no."

Laíki pointed and looked at Mamoúd. The Egyptian went over, hugged and kissed Jacob like a relative would. Jacob lifted Laíki and gave him a long kiss on each cheek. The stubble of beard made the boy wince but he was happy to find his favorite uncle.

With Laíki in Jacob's arms, the three slowly wandered to a far end of the prison where no one gathered. They saw the car and Jacob was overjoyed seeing his brother, Isaac, sitting in the front seat. Nobody waved.

Quickly Pepo ran over to the fence. With Mamoúd on one side and Pepo on the other, their strong bodies lifted the bottom of the fence until it was high enough for Laíki and Jacob to crawl under. Mamoúd followed, and just as quickly, they ran to the car. Everyone stumbled in and Mamoúd drove off.

Laíki could now welcome his uncle with words as well as hugs.

A GOLD MEDAL COMES HOME

The family had a huge celebration in honor of Jacob's return. Friends and neighbors who had heard of the trouble came to the large dinner. And it was Laíki who was the hero.

Jacob entertained them with his misadventures: How an elderly couple shared food with him on the boat; how the fishing boat stopped working near the Greek island of Samos, and they had to wait and transfer to another boat; how long it took in Turkish custody; and finally, how someone overheard him speak Greek and then his arrest by the British.

Laíki loved listening to his uncle and he had the best seat in the house at dinner—Jacob's lap!

Besides kissing and hugging his nephew, Jacob whispered in the child's ear, "Pashá, I have a surprise for you. I did not need to use your father's medal."

And with that, he pulled the medal out of his pocket and handed it to his nephew. Laíki hugged his uncle and quickly ran from the room yelling, "Papa, look what Uncle Jacob brought for me!" Isaac and Jacob laughed, as did the rest of the party.

Laíki ran to his room, found the colorful bag, and slowly put the somewhat dull gold piece safely in its place.

"I will polish it first thing in the morning" he thought, "and keep it forever."

A Medal Comes Home

MEDALS BETTER LEFT NOT WON

I have wondered for a long time what my uncle Isaac Cohen might have accomplished if he had actually entered the Olympic competitions in 1932 and, especially, if he went to the 1936 Olympics that were held in Berlin, Germany.

My uncle, well known in Greece, might have become a better-known athlete world wide…a Jewish athlete none-the-less.

As the Nazis overwhelmed most of Europe, would he have been an easier target because of his fame? Other Jewish Olympic athletes in countries under Nazi control were caught in the web and sent to concentration camps. Few survived.

Would my uncle and his family have come to the same fate if he had competed? I don't know but I am so very glad that he didn't. I would never have gotten to meet one of the most courageous men I have ever met. And, his story would never have been told.

The Cohen Family—1940

TEN GOLD MEDALS—UPDATE

What you just read is a true story of how part of my family escaped the Holocaust in Greece. Others in the family survived concentration camps. Many, many perished.

My uncle Isaac followed his trade after coming to Israel, selling dry goods. He died in 2000. Dora Albala Cohen, unfortunately, passed away just before the publication of this book.

Laíki owns his own unique lamp establishment. He married and has children and grandchildren. Little Joya became a hair stylist in Israel. A grown Laíki appears in my film WE ARE NOT ALONE: GREEK JEWS & THE HOLOCAUST.

Jacob Cohen became a photographer in Israel. He married and had children and grandchildren. He passed away in 1982.

Of the rescuers, Dr. Kostas Nikoláou was honored by Yad Vashem in Israel, given the title of "Righteous Among Nations" for his role as a rescuer, and just recently, by the Anti-Defamation League in New York City with their "Courage To Care" award. I kept in touch with the Good Doctor for many years after locating him in a suburb of Athens in 1987. We honored him continuously by remembering his birthday, sending him greetings on holidays, and either calling or visiting whenever my wife, Diana, and I were in Greece.

I remember, it was December of 2002, and Diana and I were touring Greece. When we finally got to Athens, I decided to call his home only to hear crying at the other end of the phone line. Through the tears, the family told me that Kostas had died just the week before. Just the week before! We cried too. We were just as stunned and saddened as the family was.

The only photo we have of the baker and his wife is the one in the book. We continue to search for them, hoping that one day their family will read this and find us. I would very much like to say thank you.

Avierinós, whose real name was Vasílis Perséidis, became a farmer near Marathona after the war, even though he had studied to be a lawyer. The Cohens knew him only by his code name, and it was not until 1990 that the family asked Doctor Nikoláou to look for him in Greece.

It turned out that Vasílis and Kostas were friends, neither knowing of each other's underground activities. That's how we befriended Vasílis and brought him to Israel to meet with the family he had saved.

Vasílis was honored by a synagogue in Washington, DC and was included in a short film about how the Cohens and others were saved on Évvoia. He appears in an earlier film of rescue by Sy Rotter, IT WAS NOTHING, IT WAS EVERYTHING. Vasílis was also honored by the Association of Friends of Greek Jewry in the summer of 2000 in a beautiful ceremony in Athens where he was given the Association's Award of Moral Courage.

Sadly, Vasílis just died in June, 2004.

Except for the baker Panayotarákos, we have stayed in touch with the families of the rescuers as well as the succeeding generations of my own family.

This has been a joyous story, unlike many other sad stories that the Holocaust has heaped upon Jews and others who were different. Even now, many years after the Holocaust, we still need to learn our lessons. We certainly don't want it to happen again.

Isaac Dostis
October 2004

THE FAMILY TREE OF ISAAC DOSTIS

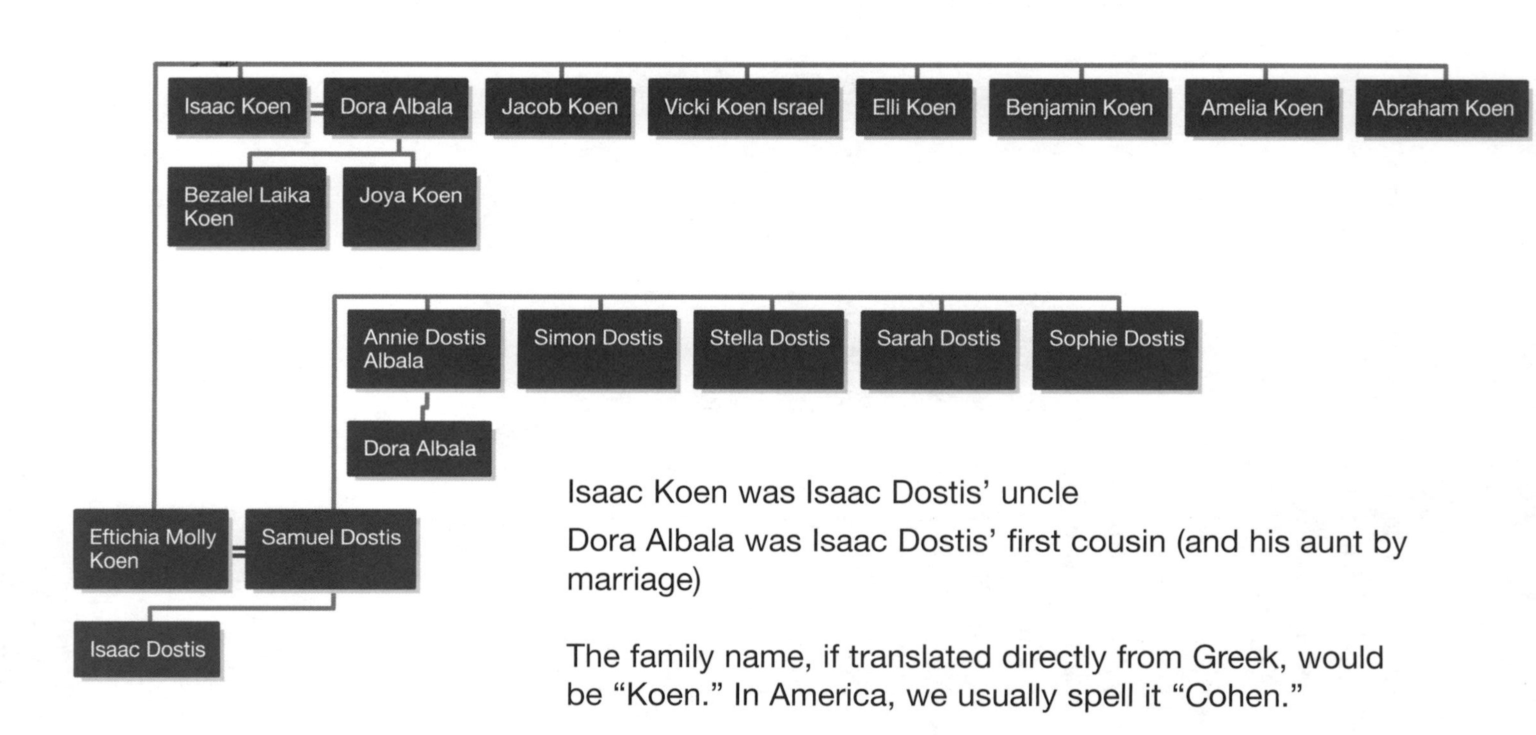

Isaac Koen was Isaac Dostis' uncle

Dora Albala was Isaac Dostis' first cousin (and his aunt by marriage)

The family name, if translated directly from Greek, would be "Koen." In America, we usually spell it "Cohen."

PHOTOGRAPHS

Isaac Cohen throwing the Javelin

Isaac Cohen holding the leadership flag

Isaac Cohen at the finish line

1944 Turkey Escape
Greek Jews celebrate escape from Nazis. Isaac Cohen—third on right Laíki Cohen—in front of checkered tablecloth
Dora Cohen—third on left Joya Cohen—fifth on left behind French captain

Cohen family c. 1940

Cohen family on the run

Isaac Cohen with Kostas Nickolaou in Athens

Jacob Cohen

Vassilis Pereidis, Israel, 1996

REVIEWS

"Circumstances and good luck notwithstanding, this is a story of moral choices, familial love, and innocent children learning what it takes to survive. A well-written and eminently useful tale."

—Sy Siegler, Director Holocaust Center
Brookdale Community College, NJ

"This is an important and moving story of the Cohens, one Greek Jewish family, and their successful battle to survive in the midst of the Nazi Occupation of their country. It is a beautiful portrait, not only of their courage, but also their heroism and fundamental decency of the many Greeks from all walks of life who risked their lives so that this family could survive. An important story for youngsters to read."

—Anita Altman, Deputy Managing Director
United Jewish Appeal

"Ten Gold Medals: Glory or Freedom, a true family adventure, is told in an interesting and compelling manner while highlighting the subjects of Greek Jewry and the Holocaust, the Righteous Christians in Greek history and universal family values. This work will shed light in an under-explored corner of Judeo/Greco history and will certainly stimulate a dialogue about this little-known area of Holocaust studies among the young people fortunate enough to read it."

—Vincent Giordano
Creator of the "Before The Flame Goes Out" project documenting the Romaniote Jews of Ioannina Greece.

"I loved the story sooo much! I plan to get a copy as soon as it comes out."

—Jessica Fagel
Temple Isaiah of Great Neck Hebrew School
Student

"Ten Gold Medals was a great Jewish story and with every medal I was left wanting more. The story was deep and if someone reads it and just gets the outside or doesn't get it at all, then he missed out on a lot."

—Daniel Sofferman
Temple Isaiah of Great Neck Hebrew School
Student

TITLES OF RELATED INTEREST

This book is the latest in a series of books on the Jews of Greece published by Bloch Publishing. **Ten Gold Medals: Glory or Freedom** is the second book in the series published for the Association of Friends of Greek Jewry. The first was **Yannina-Journey To the Past.**

In addition, Bloch Publishing has also published ***The Holocaust in Salonika: Eyewitness Accounts*** and ***A Liter of Soup and Sixty Grams of Bread*** for Sephardic House as part of their Greek Holocaust Memoirs and Studies Series.

Additional books are planned in the future, both by The Association of Friends of Greek Jewry and Sephardic House.